# APRIL IS FOR ASHER
## MOUNTAIN MEN OF MUSTANG MOUNTAIN

KACI ROSE

Copyright © 2023, by Kaci Rose, Five Little Roses Publishing. All Rights Reserved.

No part of this publication may be reproduced, distributed, or transmitted in any form or by any means, including photocopying, recording, or other electronic or mechanical methods, or by any information storage and retrieval system without the prior written permission of the publisher, except in the case of very brief quotations embodied in critical reviews and certain other noncommercial uses permitted by copyright law.

Publisher's Note: This is a work of fiction. Names, characters, places, and incidents are a product of the author's imagination. Locales and public names are sometimes used for atmospheric purposes. Any resemblance to actual people, living or dead, or to businesses, companies, events, institutions, or locales is completely coincidental.

Book Cover By: Kelly Lambert-Greer

Editing By: Debbe @ **On The Page, Author and PA Services**

*To the Match of the Month Patrons, especially...*

**Jackie Ziegler**

*And to our supporters on Kickstarter, especially...*

**Ashley Coonfield who named Wild Lightning**

*Thank you so much for your support. We couldn't do what we love without you!*

# CHAPTER 1
# ASHER

"DAMMIT, RUBY!" I bite out as I pay for my to-go coffee.

"Oh, hush you. I'm three for three and it's your turn!" She swats at me playfully with her bright red manicured nails, only I'm not playing.

"I don't want my picture and information plastered all over the town website!" I tell her, trying to make her understand I'm not kidding.

This is the fourth month in a row she's done this. Now, with Miles and Kinley getting together, I fear she won't ever stop. None of us mountain men want to be in the spotlight and featured on the town website for everyone to see. There is a reason we moved to the mountain, and it wasn't to be closer to people.

"Come on, look at Jackson, Ford, and Miles over there. They are so happy. I just want that for you too and the rest of the Mustang Mountain Riders," she says, referring to the motorcycle club the guys and I are in.

I glance outside where the guys are waiting on me with their girls. They are happy, but I don't know how much of that Ruby had to do with it. Ford and Luna have known each other since they were kids, and Miles's girl literally jumped in his car out of nowhere. Jackson's with Miles's younger sister. So, unless Ruby controls all things, she can't take credit for that, but I won't fight with her. Not here like this, anyway.

The guys and I keep saying we will talk to her, but one thing after another comes up. Though it's now just moved to the top of my priority list.

"Take it down. You had your fun." I point at her to get her attention and leave the money for the coffee as I grabbed my to-go cup and headed out the door.

At least I won't be the only single guy at the meeting today. Miles was able to grab Jonas and his brother Jensen, too. I love these guys, but I wasn't thrilled to be doing wedding planning stuff. Even if it's for these men who I'd do anything for. If I had to guess, they needed pure manpower today to see what could be accomplished. I'm not sure because I zoned out when the wedding talk started.

"By the look on your face, I guess you saw you are Mr. April?" Luna cringes.

"You knew?" I growl, and Ford gives me a look that says to knock it off. We may be brothers in arms, but he will protect his girl to the end.

"It just hit our emails while you were inside. I'm

pretty sure us here in town are the last notified when it goes up," Emma says with a sad smile.

Of course, we are getting it out far and wide first because she knows we won't be happy. She is a smart, old bird. I will give her that.

"Great," I mumble just as my phone rings.

Answering it, I find my dispatcher at the mustang refuge on the other line. She's a volunteer and works from home. The sound of her baby crying fills the background as well.

"Asher we just got a call that there is a horse, they think one of the wild mustangs that was hit by a car. It's still alive." She goes on to give me the information and says she already has one of the volunteers on their way with the trailer for transport.

"There is a horse that has been hit on the side of the road. I'm going to need some help," I tell the guys.

"We are in," Jensen says and nods to Jonas. Any reason to get out of this wedding stuff, I'm sure, and I can't blame them.

"Well, the girls can come with us and you two can go help too," Miles says.

Jackson and Ford nod as we head out.

"Perfect let's go," I say and we waste no time getting in my truck and following the directions my dispatcher texted me.

The directions lead us into the base of the mountains where the mustangs like to run. Not that we could miss it. There are no less than eight cars pulled over and a number of people surrounding the horse, which is only stressing her out.

"Come on guys, do you want people crowding you when you are injured? Back the fuck up," I tell them, not giving a shit who I offend. I come from the rodeo circuit, and they cuss worse than a cowboy with a nail through his boot. Most of these people are tourists, probably on their way to Glacier National Park. The locals know better and give wild animals plenty of room.

The guys and I get to work. They have helped me many times and jump right into it. Ford goes right to crowd control and gets them back across the street and away from the horse to give her and me some room.

Jackson, who has a way with animals, starts working on calming her down. Right now, she seems mostly dazed and confused. Jensen jumps up to help guide my volunteer with the trailer in place as I assess the mare's injuries with Jonas's help.

Even though I've been a large animal vet for several years, it never gets easier seeing them like this. I have to put my emotions aside and focus on the animal and what's best for her.

Without a doubt, she's been hit by a car and has many open cuts and a lot of blood, but I don't think it's anything from which she can't recover. But I need to get her back to the refuge where my clinic is and get her tranquilized and calm to really get a look. She is one of the wild mustangs and is afraid of people.

Giving her a mild sedative, I want to help her relax enough to hopefully get her in the trailer.

Almost two hours later, we finally get her stable and back to the refuge and I'm able to look her over.

"How bad is it?" Jensen asks.

"I need an x-ray to check for internal injuries, but the external ones look worse than they are. It's a lot of blood, but so long as we stop any infection, they aren't an issue. Just a few stitches," I tell him.

The guys stick around to help because moving a knocked-out horse around isn't easy. But we get all the tests done we need to. Thankfully, there is nothing going on inside other than some bruising, which is to be expected.

"She was extremely lucky. I bet she ran into the street and the car tried to stop. It couldn't have been going too fast, or have a lot more injuries," I tell them. After we get her settled in her recovery stall, we wait for one of the volunteers to get here to watch over her.

When she wakes up, she might hurt herself because she won't know where she is and could go into defense mode. We want to make sure that doesn't happen. Also, we also want to make sure she doesn't have an adverse reaction to any of the medications we give her.

Watching her while she is out, she seems so peaceful, and it reminds me why I do what I do. I love helping these horses, and I never regret the day that I made Mustang Mountain my home.

Once the volunteer comes to relieve me, I finally go

back to my office to drink my now very cold cup of coffee and get the paperwork on this animal done. But I get stopped on the way as I always seem to do.

"Asher, there's a woman here asking to speak to you," Donna, my receptionist, says.

We get people in all the time wanting to talk to the owner about this event or media coverage. Charles is my PR guy and has taken over a lot of the event planning and social media, too.

"Have her talk to Charles. I need to get the report going on that horse we just brought in," I tell her.

"No, thank you. That won't do because Charles isn't the father of my baby," a woman says with a voice I could never forget.

That voice haunts me in my sleep, taunting me that I'd never see her again.

"Jenna?" I ask in shock as I turned to face her.

She looks a bit paler, and a lot more tired than the last time I saw her, but it is Jenna, the face I see every night when I go to sleep.

"Glad you remember me," she says, softer this time.

Then what she said hits me.

"Did you just say father of your baby?" I ask in shock.

"Yes," she says, raising her chin and suddenly it's like someone punched me in the gut.

"Let's go into my office," I say, looking over at Donna, who rivals Ruby as the town gossip.

Thankfully, Jenna follows me into my office and

takes a seat. After closing the door, I collapse into my chair as I process what she has told me.

"Pregnant" is the only word I could get out.

"Yes, I'm about four months along. But I didn't know how to contact you or where to find you until I saw the 'Mustang Mountain Man of the Month' post this morning. Since I believe you have the right to know, I took the day off work and came down to see you. I want nothing from you..."

"Whoa, stop. Information overload," I say and rest my head in my hands and rub my temples.

Jenna and I had one amazing and perfect night together at the bar in Whitefish for a Bachelorette party. A few of the guys and I were there for a charity MC ride. We spent the night drinking, dancing, and talking.

Then we ended up back at my hotel room and had the best night of sex mixed with more talking, and a late night food run. Just before dawn, we passed out. When I woke up, she was gone. Even though I tried to track her down, I found nothing.

Now I find out that our perfect night together has produced a child and has tied me to this woman forever. The universe sure has a sense of humor.

"First, do you need something to eat or drink?" I offer her.

"I'm good. I have some water with me, but I could use a restroom if you have one," she says.

"Yes, out the door to the left, then first door on your

left." I tell her and thankfully she leaves her bag, so I know she is coming back.

I don't plan to let her slip away again without a way to contact her and not just because she is carrying my child.

Then I start to process what she just said. She's almost four months pregnant, which lines up with the night we were together, and she found me from Ruby's bachelor post. I don't want to encourage Ruby, but I could give her a huge kiss right now because she brought this girl back to me.

Did she really say she wants nothing from me? That's fine. She can want nothing, but she will be getting everything. There is no way a kid of mine is walking around on this earth without me in their life. And there is no way Jenna is getting away again.

By the time she rejoins me, I'm a lot calmer and thinking straighter.

## CHAPTER 2
# JENNA

I TAKE an extra moment in the bathroom to regain my composure. Seeing him today really knocked me for a more of a loop than I expected. He didn't slam the door in my face, so to speak, so that's a good thing, right?

Placing my hand on my stomach that is just starting to 'pop' as my sister calls it, I remind myself I am doing this for my little one. Even if Asher isn't a part of our lives, he has a right to know. I want to be able to look my child in the eye and say I did everything I could as his or her mom.

The problem is, I know even when a father is around, it doesn't mean he will be there for the kid. My father was married to Mom and lived with us, but he wasn't there for simple things like dinner or the bigger things like my school plays, or when I broke my arm. When my sister was sick, he was barely there. My mom shouldered all of that, and all my dad contributed was a paycheck. I want more for my kid.

With a final deep breath, I go back to his office, walking slower than normal, before closing the door behind me and taking my seat again.

"I'm glad you found me. I really thought we had a connection, and then I wake up the next morning and you were gone," he says.

Even though he's watching my every move, it doesn't feel creepy. I thought I was the only one who felt we had a connection, but I know how one-night stands go. You say things in the heat of the moment, but then go your separate ways in the morning. It's why the thought never appealed much to me, but things seemed different in the lights of a Bachelorette party, drinking, and peer pressure added in.

I'd never done anything like that before and I thought with the alcohol and all I was just imagining what I felt between us. But hearing him say that he felt it too pulls at my heart.

Giving myself a mental shake, I realize that this isn't about just me anymore. I have to do what is best for this baby. Nothing or nobody will distract me from taking care of my baby.

"I know how one-night stands are. You say things, but it all looks different in the morning. Besides, I had an interview to go to." I try to brush it off.

His expression doesn't change, making him very hard to read.

"I remember you told me you are up for a big promotion. How did the interview go?" he asks, leaning forward and resting his elbows on the desk.

His whiskey brown eyes get more serious than they were earlier and his muscles cause the long sleep shirt he is wearing to stretch across his arms and chest.

I remember what it's like to have those strong arms cage me in while he was on top of me and how safe I felt. Instead of feeling trapped, I truly enjoyed it.

*Dammit Jenna, stop thinking about that night.*

As he waits for my answer, he gives me a cocky half smile, almost like he knows where my thoughts were just now.

"Good. I made it to the next round of interviews and was offered the job last week."

"I knew you'd get it! I'm so excited for you!" He seems truly happy for me as a huge smile crosses his face.

As I start to relax, he looks at out the window and then back at me. The look on his face is more serious this time.

"But let's make one thing clear, we may have started that night looking for a one-night stand, but we both know that night turned into so much more. The universe has made that perfectly clear." He looks down at my belly and I place a protective hand over our little one.

"It doesn't matter. This job means a promotion and a move to Billings. By this time next month, I will be halfway across the state." I tell him and watch the muscle in his jaw tick.

There. Tell him, and it's like ripping a Band-Aid

off. Get everything out there and in the open, I think to myself.

"There is no world where I'm not going to be involved in my child's life, Jenna," he says softly.

But I can tell he isn't joking around either. "I don't want anything from you, and am prepared to raise this kid on my own. The promotion comes with a great pay raise, and I was already making good money. Right now, the only tricky part of the move is putting my house up for sale and finding a place to live in Billings. I'll be doing it before the baby gets here."

What he doesn't need to know is I already put my house up for sale and have been looking at places in Billings. Nor do I need to tell him how much it's all stressing me out.

"Give me a chance to be involved. I will prove I'm going to be a hands-on dad and a good one," he all but begs, the vulnerability in his voice pulls at my heart-strings.

Though I expected him to be relieved that I didn't want anything from him. Also, I expected him to just walk away. Most guys from a one-night stand want nothing to do with a child. At least what I had seen from my friends. Until Asher, I've never done the one-night stand thing.

"I have a doctor appointment in a few days..." I start, but I don't even get to finish my sentence.

"I will be there. Let me see your phone. I'm going to put in my number, the number here, and a few of my friends' numbers, so you are always able to reach me no matter what," he says, shocking me yet again.

He holds his hand out and waits patiently while I process everything he just said. I reach for my bag and search through it to find my phone that has shifted to the bottom. After unlocking it, I hand it to him.

Right away, he starts entering his number.

"I'm putting my cell, my house number, and the number here at the refuge with the extension that takes you right to my desk. Also, I'm adding in Jackson, Ford, and Miles numbers. Now that they are engaged, they are free a lot. If I'm out, I'm normally with one of them, or they will know where to find me."

My head spins with all the information he's giving me.

"I'm texting myself, so I have your number too," he says, with his fingers flying across my phone screen.

His phone beeps, and he is still typing on my phone. I start to wonder what he's doing and start to second guess giving him my phone over when he hands it back.

"You didn't have to do that," I tell him, looking at what he entered into my phone.

It was just the contacts he mentioned, along with a text to himself. He really wants to be reachable to offer six ways to get a hold of him.

When he pulls out his phone, I'm guessing to save my phone number.

"When and where is the doctor appointment so I

can put it on my calendar right now," he says, looking up at me.

I give him the.

After entering the date and doctor info for next week, he says, "I will have to move a meeting with Charles."

My heart sinks. Why did I get my hopes up that he'd actually be there?

I've been to every doctor appointment alone. Everyone else there has the baby's dad with them. I always get looks. One girl is a surrogate and both the baby's parents are there.

Even though it sucks, I smile and push through it. Part of me was hoping to have Asher at my side this time, but no such luck, I guess.

"That's okay, you don't have to be there," I try to hide my disappointment.

He sets his phone down and looks me right in the eyes for a moment before speaking.

"I will be there. I'm sorry I was just thinking out loud," he says.

"You don't have to move a meeting around, it's just..."

"I will be there. There is no way I'd miss it," he says. There is an adamant tone in his voice, and I know without a doubt he will be there. I'm not sure how I know it, but he means what he says and his words mean something.

Though right now, he seems determined, but will he be this committed to be in his kid's life when he has to drive several hours one way to Billings? Probably not.

"After the appointment, I'd like to take you to lunch so we can discuss things. Like me visiting on the weekends and all when you move," he says, but he seems angry at the same time.

He has a life here and with what little I know about the refuge, I doubt he will be getting away every weekend. So what can it hurt to let him make plans? Plans are easy to break and I'm not going to pass up food.

"That's fine. Just no Chinese food or burgers. The smell of both makes me sick right now."

"Oh, I will find something. There is plenty to eat in Whitefish," he says.

I need to be careful around this man, as I can tell he'd be easy to believe and easy to lose my heart to him.

## CHAPTER 3
## ASHER

I CALL the guys to a meeting at our MC club house. It used to be a brothel back in its Wild West days. A couple renovated it and tried to turn it into a museum back in the '80s, but it's too far off the beaten path. It didn't do well, so it sat around empty until we all bought it.

The sordid history is what drove us to it. After renovating it, we used the large old bar downstairs mostly for meetings and hanging out. We haven't done much restoration upstairs. Per the town's historical society, we have to keep it true to its time period so the project's been on hold.

It wasn't a big deal because The Mustang Mountain Riders was originally to be men's only meeting place with the exception of Ford's daughter Izzy. But the rule changed because three of the guys are now engaged. Emma, Luna, and Kinley are the only women allowed in. They don't seem to mind the space, though they are hinting to renovate a room upstairs for them to use when we meet.

As she likes to remind us, Ford's daughter Izzy is the club princess. We turned the old office off the bar into her personal playroom. Thankfully, by the time everyone shows up, she is entertained and having fun.

Glancing around, I look at the eleven guys in front of me. Some are newer to the club like Ace, and others have been around for a while and have been my support system. If I'm going to make it through this, I know I'm going to need every one of them.

Taking a deep breath, I launch into the full story.

"Remember that charity ride we did a few months ago in Whitefish?" Not all the guys were able to go to it, but we all promoted it and donated money.

"Yeah, the one we froze our asses off and then ended up staying overnight. We went to the bar down the road where a bachelorette party was taking place," Jensen says, smirking.

"Yeah. You met that woman you haven't shut up about. But she was gone the next morning." Jensen's brother Jonas says.

"That's the one. Well, that woman's name is Jenna, and she showed up at the refugee yesterday," I tell them. Then let it sink in before I drop the next bombshell.

"She found you?" Luna asks, shocked.

I almost feel bad for keeping the most surprising news back.

"Yep, thanks to Ruby's little Mr. April ad. And

that's not all." I shake my head in disbelief that I'm about to say these words.

I can see it on the faces of a few of my brother's-in-arms. They know something big is coming.

"She's pregnant, just got a job promotion, and plans to move to Billings once she gets her housing sorted out."

They all sit there in complete silence until Ford clears his throat.

"What did she want by reaching out?" he asks.

"That's it. She didn't want anything. She's going to raise the baby on her own but wanted to do the right thing and let me, as the father, know."

The room is so quiet you can hear the clinking of Izzy's toys from her playroom.

"I hate to be the one to ask this, but are you sure the baby is yours?" Luna asks.

"That night, the connection we had was something that I have never felt before. We talked a lot. Not only has she never done the one-night stand before, but until that night, she hadn't been with anyone in a year. She doesn't strike me as someone to sleep around, so my gut is saying, yeah, it is."

"Still, you should get a DNA test and talk to a lawyer. You have rights, including visitation if you want them," Ace says, whipping out his phone and grabbing a pen and paper.

"Damn right I want them. There is no way I'm turning my back on my kid." I tell them.

They all nod, and I know they will have my back

any way I need. I also know any kid of mine will be treated as one of their own, just like they do Izzy.

"I figured. Listen, here is the name of a lawyer. He's a good guy, a mountain man like us, and only does pro bono work for those that need it. If he can't help, he can give you the name of someone who can. His name is Jack, and he lives just outside Helena in Whiskey River," Ace says, handing me the paper with Jack's info. Even though I put it in my wallet, I hate to think I might have to go that route.

"Next week she has a doctor appointment and is letting me go and be involved. So I want to see how that is going to play out first. If I don't have to. I don't want to spook her."

What I don't tell them is I want more than just rights to my kid, I want Jenna too. If I get lawyers involved from day one, I won't get that. First, I need to build trust with her and take things slow. Though not too slow, we only have five months before the baby will be here.

I'M early to the doctor's appointment. Since I hadn't been to the doctor's office before, I left really early, so I had plenty of time to find it. Now I'm just waiting for her to get here. I'm equally excited to see Jenna and take her to lunch, as I am to know more about our baby.

While I don't know what to expect at this doctor's appointment, I have been doing some research. Probably very soon we will be able to find out if it's a boy or girl and today we might even get to hear the baby's heartbeat. That alone both excites and terrifies me.

When Jenna arrives, parking next to me, I breathe a sigh of relief. Having my eyes on her and knowing her and the baby are okay calms me.

Well, that is, until she gets out of the car and I see the stress all over her face.

"What's wrong?" I ask.

"It's been a week already, and it's only Tuesday. If you still want to go, we can talk at lunch," she says.

I've been looking forward to our lunch all week, but even more so now. There is no way I'd let her out of it now.

"Of course I want to go. I found a few places and you can pick when we are done." Placing my hand on her lower back, I lead her into the doctor's office.

Being so close, I can smell the perfume she is wearing. It's the same one she wore the night we were together and my dick suddenly thinks it's time to come out and play.

Great, the last thing I need is to walk in to the doctor's office with a hard on. Especially since that is what got us in here to begin with.

We don't wait near as long as I expect before we are called to the back. They check her weight and have her pee in a cup. My job is being put in charge of holding her jacket and purse in the hallway. Then we get shown to the exam room where Jenna sits on the exam table and I sit in the chair next to her. When the nurse takes her vitals, she frowns and retakes them.

"What's wrong?" I ask, as they share a look of understanding.

"They are a bit high..." the nurse says.

"It's just the stress from this morning," Jenna dismisses it. But the nurse gives her a tense smile.

"Well, the doctor will be right in to talk to you," she says, scurrying out of the room.

With the back of the exam table up, Jenna lies back in a reclined position and looks over at me. The lack of sleep is evident around her eyes, and she looks pale but still as beautiful as that first night I saw her.

Reaching out, I brush some hair from her face and run my thumb over her cheek. For a moment, we lock eyes and enjoy each other's touch before there is a knock, and the doctor walks in.

"Alright mom is this Dad?" she asks.

"Yes." Jenna smiles at me and just hearing them refer to me as dad does something funny with my heart.

"Your vitals are a bit high, so I'd like to recheck them again before you leave," the doctor says.

Nodding, Jenna says, "I've been stressed about this move."

"I get it. Moves are stressful under the best of situations, and we know this isn't the best of circumstances. Make sure you are resting and taking down time since you are still working. Now let's get your measurements, and then we will listen to the baby."

The doctor pulls out a small tape measure and starts feeling Jenna's belly before measuring it.

"Right on track. Now this gel is going to be cold," the doctor says, squeezing some on to Jenna's belly. Then she pulls out what looks like a microphone and starts running it over the gel.

It takes a moment of some weird sounds before the loud sound of a train fills the room. Jenna relaxes and reaches for my hand.

"That's your baby," the doctor says.

All I can do is stare at the tiny swell of Jenna's stomach in awe. There is a baby in there. *Our baby*.

After that, I don't hear much of what else the doctor says. In a daze, I follow Jenna out front as she makes her next appointment. Thankfully, they hand me an appointment card because I couldn't remember the day and time to save my life.

Once the cold air hits me in the parking lot, I snap back into action. The mother of my child needs to eat, which means my child needs to eat.

"There is a deli with soups and sandwiches nearby. Also, there's a little Italian café, and a Mexican place all within walking distance." I point each out in the plaza which is nearby.

"You really did do your research, huh? Italian sounds great," she says, smiling at me.

We walk across the street and once we are seated and have placed our order, I finally look at her.

"Why are you so stressed out?" I ask.

"Remember, I told you I put my house on the market?"

Nodding, I wait for her to go on as my mind races. Does her place need work? The guys and I can go over in a weekend and fix up anything she needs done.

"Well, a couple from out-of-state put in an offer over the asking price. It was all cash, but I have to move out this weekend. They need to move in next week for his job. Not wanting to pass up an extra twenty thousand dollars, I took the offer."

While she's stressed about telling me she's moving sooner, my heart sinks because I'm losing time with her.

"Well, the place I rented in Billings won't be ready for another six weeks, and I have to finish training my replacement at my job here before they will transfer me. On Sunday, I could move in with my sister because I can't live in my place with everything in boxes."

She's stressed, but I'm relieved she isn't leaving just yet. As I listen to her speak, I'm trying to find a way I can help relieve her stress.

"It would be a great solution, except she's newly married. They will be keeping me up all hours of the night with loud sex and thin walls. Plus, she has a cat and I'm allergic to cats. For six more weeks, it's just not going to work."

"Move in with me." The works are out of my mouth before I can stop them. But the more I think about it, the more I love the idea.

"Don't be crazy. I can't do that," she says, waving me off.

"Why not? You work up the street, right? Today it took me thirty minutes to get here. You'd have your own room, and no cats which having an allergic reaction could cause harm to the baby. There's an entire section in the baby book stating that pregnant women shouldn't even be around cat litter. You'll have your own personal craving fetcher, and if at any point you aren't feeling well or don't want to even make the drive into work, I can take you, or anyone of my friends or their fiancés can."

After I lay it all out on the table, she stares at me with a funny look on her face. Holding my breath, I'm hoping she'll say yes. But I don't get any answer because the server brings our food.

Before she takes her first bite, she says, "It's just temporary until my place in Billings is ready. Though I insist on paying rent."

"No, I don't have a mortgage on the place. There's no way I'm making money off of you. Any money you save will be for the baby. If you want to help with cooking or cleaning, or hell, even decorating the place, I won't say no."

Taking a bite of lasagna, I can see she's thinking out as she eats.

"Then, if you let me pitch in for groceries, you have yourself a deal."

If it gets Jenna in my house for the next six weeks, I can concede on groceries.

## CHAPTER 4
## JENNA

AS I STARE at all the people in my living room, I'm still in shock. Not only did Asher show up this morning, but he brought three couples with him and several other guys, all with trucks. I can't remember all the names, but they are hard workers.

The women have been super sweet and treat me like I'm their best friend. They have been helping me pack up what I haven't gotten to yet. The guys are loading boxes and furniture to go to storage and have already made one trip taking a bunch of stuff.

"Okay, so what do you want to do with the food that is left in the kitchen?" Emma asks, sitting beside me on the couch where Asher insisted I put my feet up and rest.

He's told everyone the couch will be the last thing to go and they agree. Apparently, they all know about my doctor visit and how stressed I was, too. They have all been checking on me, making sure I have water and snacks. When I got up to pee earlier, the two guys in the room surrounded me, asking what I needed and telling me to sit back down.

Though when I told them I was just going to the bathroom, they backed off, and the girls started giggling. It's been great to laugh today, and more than once. Unfortunately, it seems like it's been a long time since I've been so carefree and relaxed.

"I'll take the food she isn't taking with her," my sister says, walking in the door.

This morning she had a hair appointment and said she'd stop by after. She wanted to meet Asher and help me pack because neither of us expected this kind of turn out.

"Nothing will go to waste at your house. There you go," I say, handing the food to my sister. Oh, by the way, that's my sister Hailey. Hailey, this is Emma."

"Ok sis, which one of these hunky bearded muscle men walking around here is yours? Damn, if I had known what Mustang Mountain was hiding, I'd have hung out here a lot more," my sister says, eying the men walking in and out of my front door.

"Mumm. Asher?" When I don't see him, I call out and he steps out of the hallway where they were dismantling my bed.

"You, okay?" He asks, his eyes looking me over and then looking at the people around me. When he sees a woman he doesn't know standing over me, he tenses up.

"This is my sister Hailey. She wanted to meet you.

Well actually, you met her that night at the bachelorette party, but she wanted to officially meet you," I ramble.

"I figured it was time, since it looks like you will be in her life for at least the next eighteen years, if not longer," my sister says.

She has been my biggest support system. Not only did she buy my pregnancy test, she stayed while I took the test and it came back positive. While I cried and explained how I got pregnant from my one and only one-night stand, she was the one to hold me. Then she helped me research OB/GYNs in the area and make doctor appointments. She has even been reading the baby books with me and helping me with this move.

"Nice to meet you. Jenna has all great things to say about you. Thank you for helping her when I couldn't be there," he says genuinely.

That seems to soften my sister, who was determined to have a wall up against him. But just like he does with me, he seems to break it down pretty damn fast.

"Who are all these people?" She asks when two guys walk by carrying my dresser outside.

"They are my friends. When I told them about her last doctor appointment and everything with the move, they all said they would be here to help clear and clean her place, so it's ready for closing on Monday," Asher says.

"Wow. Well, where can I jump in?" Hailey says, rolling up her sleeves, ready to dive in.

"We are clearing out her bedroom now and it will be ready to clean if you want to start there," Asher says.

He has been directing everything today. When Hailey looks at me, I just shrug.

"My orders are not to get up from the couch, so I've been letting him handle it. Everything going to his place is already loaded into his truck and one of the other guy's trucks. Now we are clearing and sorting everything. Either they go out to trash, storage, or donating," I tell her.

"I like this much more laid back version of you. If it takes him to bring it out of you, then I approve," Hailey says. Then goes toward my bedroom without letting me say a word.

"Lunch has arrived!" Izzy announces, running into the house.

Ford, Luna, Izzy, and Kinley went to get food for everyone. After they bringing it in, all the guys gather around the kitchen. Though no one touches anything as Luna lays items on the counter.

All the burgers smell amazing. For a week the smell of burgers made me throw up and now I am craving them. Pregnancy is wild.

"Okay, here is your burger, Jenna. Let me grab your fries and a drink. Do you need ketchup or anything?" Luna says, handing me food.

From the hallway, my sister is watching how everyone is taking care of me.

Taking the food, I put my feet down so I can eat and make more room for people to sit on the couch.

"Um, yes, thank you. If you could get me ketchup and some napkins, that would be great. There should be some above the fridge," I tell her.

After bringing the ketchup and napkins back, Luna asks, "You have everything?" She looks at the boxes in front of me I am using as a makeshift table.

"Yep, I'm good." I tell her, unwrapping the burger.

The women get their food and Izzy's and even hand a burger to my sister. Once the girls are all sitting in the living room with me, the guys then descend into the kitchen and it's mass chaos as they grab their food.

Hailey and I look over at each other, pretty much in shock. The respect of allowing the woman to get their food first is something we have never seen before.

"Eat up, sweetheart," Asher says. Then sits on the floor next to me with a burger in one hand and fries in the other.

"Are you guys for real?" My sister says, reading my mind.

"What do you mean?" Asher asks casually as he unwraps his burger.

"They all waited until the girls had their food. They got Jenna her food first. I've never seen anything like that before in my life." Hailey says, shock clear in her voice.

"We may be rough mountain men bikers, but above all, we have respect for women and children. Common respect that all men should have, but we find many in the city don't have any more. It's why so many of us move out to the mountain. We got sick of watching how disrespectful people can be on a daily basis. We do things a lot different in Mustang Mountain. You will see," he says, and the guys quickly agree with him.

The looks of pure love on all the girls' faces say it all. This is a normal occurrence with them and not just a show they are putting on.

After lunch we finish up packing and cleaning, the girls, my sister, and I relax and talk. Every now and then we burst out laughing and their guys will stop and watch with smiles on their faces, too.

Never have I had girl friends like this. The closest I have to friends is my sister's friends because I work so much. Though I wouldn't call the people I work with friends, case in point, not one of them is here to help today.

Until now, I guess I never knew what I was missing. I really like these women. They are making plans for while I'm in town. Girls' nights, going out to the movies and other fun things. I'm finding I really can't wait.

Work has put me on reduced duty because of the pregnancy and the work transfer, so I have a ton of extra time now.

Before I know it, we are done and loading up to head back to Asher's place. Our goal is to get everything uploaded before it gets dark.

"Okay, if you need anything, you call me. Do you understand?" If this guy turns out to be a creep, I will come out no matter what time of the night." My sister whispers into my ear as she hugs me.

After I told her I was moving in with Asher a couple of days ago, she's told me this multiple times. At first, she protested but when I told her all the reasons I couldn't stay with her she was sad, but she got it. Plus, she is all for Asher being in the baby's life and wanting to be part of the pregnancy. She thinks it will make him bond with the baby more. Though she does think moving in with him is a bit extreme, but my situation right now is not normal either.

Asher has one of the other women driving my car because he insisted he drive me. He is taking this reduce all the stress thing seriously, and I'm more than happy to let him right now. Not having to think about all the logistics of the move is pretty damn calming.

That opened up a door for a whole new set of things to worry about. Like how I will survive six weeks sharing a house with him when I know what he feels like inside of me.

## CHAPTER 5
## JENNA

IT DOESN'T TAKE LONG to get to Mustang Mountain, and the town is beautiful. The only other time I was here was when I told Asher about the baby. I didn't really take it in because I was on a mission when I got there and in shock on the way home.

Asher has been quiet on the way here, letting me listen to the radio. But once we start to head up the mountain, he turns it down.

"This weekend, I will check out your car and give it a once over. I'm guessing we will need to get you some new tires to make it up and down the mountain. While the worst of the winter weather is over, we could still get a decent snow storm. If that happens, I will take you into work. Your car won't make the mountain in anything more than a couple inches of snow."

"New tires aren't cheap." I sigh, already reworking my budget for the expenses. A new baby isn't cheap, and I have the move to pay for still. I'm working myself up when he reaches out and takes me by the hand.

"Let me see what I can do. I'm friends with a mechanic in town and he owes me a favor. I bet I can get them really cheap, and Ace has helped me maintain some of the vehicles on the refuge. Maybe we can put them on in an afternoon for nothing," he squeezes my hand.

"Seriously?" I say, shocked.

"It's how things work in a small town like this. We all help each other. You will see."

When we pull up to his place, it's really nice to get out and stretch my legs. Before I can move to the porch, he's right there to help me up. Luna pulls in right behind me with my car and Ford behind her with the rest of my stuff.

"This is home." he says as we walk in, and he turns on the lights.

On the outside, it looks like a cabin in the woods. Something you might expect to see on a postcard, but newer. Yet inside, it looks like a fancy resort. There's a large stone fireplace and a state-of-the art kitchen. Beautiful, handcrafted furniture is all displayed and framed around the view out the back of his house.

"Let me give you a tour while Ford and Miles bring in your stuff," he says. Then he guides me out of the way as the guys bring in a few boxes and disappear down the hall.

"Your room is down the hall here. My room is at the end of the hall. Since I have my own bathroom, the hallway bathroom is all yours. This is my office," he says, opening the first door on our left.

It's a basic home office, but what catches my eye is the baby items stacked in the corner.

"What is all that?" I ask.

I swear a faint blush covers his cheeks.

"Well, I was researching car seats. I'm going to need one in my car and I know you haven't gotten one yet either, so I bought us each the same one so it's interchangeable. It's top of the line and rated the safest on the market right now."

I stand there in shock. For the first time, I think this man might be deadly serious about being involved in this child's life.

Stepping into his office, I look at the car seat boxes and gasp. Wow! He's picked one that's really expensive. Even though I had my eye on it, I couldn't think about buying one of them, much less two of them.

"Asher, these are too much!"

"Nothing is too much for our baby's safety. I'm not hurting for money, and I'd rather spend it on our child than myself."

"You know, I wouldn't think running a refuge would pay that much," I say, turning to face him.

Laughing, he shakes his head as he leans against the door frame.

"It doesn't. But I am a vet for large animals and that pays well. Before I settled here, I worked the rodeo circuit. I lived in a travel trailer and my expenses were minimal, traveling with the rodeo, so I saved up."

These are things you would think you'd know before having a baby with someone, but it's nice to know now. Before getting ready to leave his office, I take a look around when something on his desk catches my eye. Curiously, I walk over and pick up the stack of papers.

"What's this?" I ask. I'm staring in surprise at listings of townhouses in Billings.

"When I come visit the baby on the weekends, I have to have someplace to stay. It's more sensible than staying in a hotel. I didn't think you'd want me in your space. Besides, it's there if you need it too since you are renting," he shrugs. Like it's no big deal, but it' a very big deal. It's something you do when you are planning on a permanent change.

I don't say anything because I don't know what to say as I follow him.

"This is a spare room so we can store anything you want in here and it can be your space to do whatever. I have some stuff in the closet, but otherwise, it's all yours." He opens the bedroom door on the right, which is pretty empty other than a bookcase and a few of my boxes.

Further into the hall, he opens the bathroom door and steps back. It's bigger than my primary bath in my old place, but there is no bathtub.

"This bathroom is all yours, but if you want to have a bath, I have a clawfoot tub in my room. When I was building this cabin, Ruby insisted it would be a good way to attract a wife. If you won't tell anyone, I'll admit I've used it a few times myself."

"Who's Ruby?" I ask, thinking he's so blatantly talking about an ex-girlfriend, or hell, a current one for all I know.

"She's the mayor's wife and runs the Mercantile in town. But she's the town busybody and the one who put up the ad you saw. She likes to think of herself as mine and the guy's surrogate grandmother. Even though she drives us crazy, at the end of the day we'd do anything for her."

Moving down the hall, he opens another door. "This is your bedroom. If you need to change or move anything, just let me know and I will make it happen. My room is the door at the end of the hallway. Why don't you get settled while I make something for to eat? Do you have anything particular you'd like for dinner?"

"Well, I've got this craving for a grilled cheese," I moan. Once I say it out loud, the craving is so strong I can taste it, making my mouth water.

"You're in luck because I make a mean grilled cheese. While you relax and get settled, I will make dinner," he says. Smiling, he leaves the room, closing the door behind him.

My suitcases are on the bed, so I start there and unpack my clothes, putting them in the dresser. Finally, there's a soft knock on the door and Asher lets me know dinner is ready.

I don't know how much time has gone by, but I'm starving and my stomach is growling. When I see what he's laid out for me, I'm surprised. Not only is there a plate with grilled cheese sandwiches on the table, but a tray of French fries and a small salad. The table is set, and I'm ready to eat.

He pulls out a chair for me and I sit down, my eyes running over everything on the table in front of me.

"Go ahead and eat all you want. There are leftovers in the fridge from the other night if you're still hungry." He says, nodding toward the grilled cheese.

My eyes go wide. There is enough food here to feed me for a week. I'm not even sure that I'll be able to finish even one grilled cheese sandwich. It's the biggest grilled cheese I've ever seen. Plus, I don't know if I can even open my mouth wide enough for a bite because it's so thick.

Still, I take one and place it on my plate, along with some fries and ketchup. Then I make a small salad in the bowl he provided before reaching for my sandwich.

He watches me take a bite of the sandwich, and when I say it melts in my mouth, that doesn't even begin to describe it.

"Mm, this is the best grilled cheese I think I've ever had," I say once I've swallowed my first bite.

A huge smile crosses his face.

"I use five different cheeses and garlic butter on the bread. It's a cowboy staple from my rodeo days." He says, taking a big bite himself.

As we eat, we talk about the plans for this weekend and what our schedules for the coming week are like. Then he tells me about the refuge and how he can get calls at all hours of the night. But he assures me it's only been about once a month he gets a really late night call.

"What if you get a call and you can't get there?" I ask.

"There is a vet in town. Though she normally does small animals, she has helped out in a pinch. Also, there are a few other vets nearby who have volunteered their time and they are on the call list, too."

That makes me feel a bit better that he won't be chained to the refuge. But still, the refuge seems like it can take a lot of his time.

Once we are finished, the tiredness from the day sets in and I can't stop the huge yawn if I tried.

"Why don't you head to bed? You had a long day. Get some rest and try to sleep in. I'm just going to finish up out here and then go read."

"I think I will. It's been a long time since I've gotten to sleep in," I tell him.

Smiling, he walks me down the hall to my room.

"I'm really glad you are here," he says, running his hand down my arm before leaning in and placing a kiss to my forehead.

When he goes back toward the kitchen, I stand there stunned for a moment before walking into my room. In a daze, I get ready for bed. When I finally lie down on the bed, I just stare at the ceiling.

I think about everything Asher has done since he found out I was pregnant. He treats me better than my sister's new husband treats her. Does that mean this is all an act? How long do they say a person can put up an act before their true self starts to slip through? Six months? Great, just as the baby is born.

But even as a one-night stand when he thought he'd never see me again, he was like this. Caring and thoughtful and so damn sexy. Before I know it, I'm reliving that night all over again and I'm hot and turned on.

These pregnancy hormones are killing me! All day long, I was pretty aroused all day and now this. Looking over at the door, I can see it isn't locked. When he came to get me for dinner, he didn't walk in. Something tells me he's more of a wait to be invited in kind of guy.

What the hell. Turning off the light, I reach under the blankets, trailing my hand over my soft sweatpants. I can already feel how wet they are and I just put them on.

Sliding my hand in to my sweatpants, I barely brush my clit and have to bite my lip from moaning out loud. It feels so damn good. I want to draw it out. Though I really want to increase my pleasure, I don't want to chance getting caught. Spending all day with Asher has been teasing enough that I want to throw caution to the wind.

Picturing him above me that night, his eyes locked on mine, and the feeling of him sliding in and out of me makes me even wetter. In no time at all, my orgasm is right on the edge.

Then I focus on my clit, giving myself the perfect

amount of pressure to spiral me toward the release I'm chasing. Taking the pillow, I put in on my face just as my orgasm crashes through me, making me cry out. Hopefully, the pillow masked the sounds. After I come down, relax, and catch my breath, I move the pillow.

Staring at the ceiling, I think to myself, this is going to be a long six weeks.

I pull the pillow on my face with my other hand just as my orgasm rushes through me and I try to keep quiet.

I pull the pillow off my face and stare at the ceiling again, trying to catch my breath.

## CHAPTER 6
## ASHER

"DAMMIT!" I say as I once again hear those sexy as sin moans in my head from last night.

As I was walking by her door to go to bed, I heard her in there cry out. I had to brace my arms on the door frame to keep myself from going in there to take care of her. But I listened to every last sound until her breathing evened out and I was sure she was asleep.

Then I went to my room and took a cold shower, which didn't help. Neither did the multiple times I came in my own hand. I don't know when I fell asleep, but I know I was hard when I did.

When I slept, I dreamt of those sexy moans. The same ones she made that amazing night we had together. In my dream, I hadn't stayed outside that room and was going to get another hot and sexy night with her. Only I woke up just as I was about to slide into her.

Another cold shower and jerk off session later, I'm now trying to make us breakfast. Unfortunately, I'm painfully hard again.

"Are you okay?" Jenna's soft voice asks from behind me.

Taking a moment, I breathe deeply while willing my cock to go down. Once, I have myself under control so I don't scare her, I turn around.

"Yeah, just a rough morning. I have to head to the refuge and prepare for our annual Easter egg hunt. So I wanted to make sure I made you breakfast before I left, since you will be on your own for lunch."

Turning back to the eggs on the stove, I need to make sure I don't burn them.

"I'd like to go with you if that's okay?" she asks. Then she bites her lip like she's nervous I will say no.

"Of course, it's okay. But are you sure you don't want to stay here and relax for the day?"

"If I stay here, I will think of everything I have to do for the move, and all the things I still have to get for the baby. I will stress myself out even more. Plus, I want to see what you do and help out if I can." She shrugs like it's no big deal, but really it is.

I want her involved in my life and that fact that she is asking because she wants that too is huge for me. Also, if she is with me, I can watch out for her and make sure she isn't overdoing it.

My original plan was to send Emma or Luna out here around lunch to check on her and make sure she was okay. The problem was finding a way to make it seem like it wasn't me checking up on her.

"I'd like that. We need help stuffing all the plastic Easter eggs and you can do that sitting down with the girls and get to know each other., you can even watch a movie if you girls want. Last year, it took poor Donna three days to stuff them all on her own because she still had to answer phones while doing it. Then she took them home at night, too. She's a trooper, but I know she is happy to hand that task off this year," I tell her.

"I'd like that."

We have breakfast, get ready to go and everything is just easy. She isn't high maintenance and is practical in jeans, sneakers, and a sweater to keep warm. Though I hate that it hides her bump, but I want her comfortable too.

We walk in and are greeted by Donna.

"Well, hey there you two. The volunteers aren't here yet, but Ruby has called twice. Nothing you need to call back on," she says. Then she hands me a stack of notes of either people to call back, or emails to answer.

"Thanks Donna. I'm going to show Jenna around." I tell her not even pretending she doesn't know who Jenna is. Donna isn't ashamed of her gossip game, nor does she try to hide it, so I tend to be straight with her.

Leading Jenna back to my office, I set the papers Donna gave me on the desk.

"Here you can lock your purse in my desk, not that anyone would bother it even if you left it out."

She places her purse in the drawer, and I lock it up.

Even though I know her stuff is safe, I don't want her to worry about it even one bit.

"Let me show you around," I say. Then I hold out my hand to her, wondering if she will take it, but can't stop the smile when she does.

Taking her on a tour of my clinic, I show her where I work with the horses and the other large animals that have passed through needing to be cared for and healed.

"We had a bear get hit by a car once. Scariest thing I've ever had to do. Once we got it knocked out, I was able to treat it and then it went to the Montana Grizzly Encounter down in Bozeman. Normally it's just horses and sometime deer. Though if needed, I help with some of the local cattle, too."

As we walk down to the barn area, Hades peeks his head around the corner. We have a little bed area for him to sleep here and always leave him a bit of food and water. Jenna is so focused on the horses she doesn't see him, she just keeps on asking questions. I show her the stalls where we keep injured horses. Then we walk out the back of the barn and I show her the horses in the field.

"Our goal is to always heal and release. After tagging the animals we release, I watch them and learn about the herd. But it's a sad day when one is injured so badly they can't be released again. That is when they stay here, and they become friendlier over time. That is these guys here in this field." I stop at the barn door and load my pocket with treats.

We walk to the fence like and several of the horses see me and come over. They know I always have treats on me. It's a great way for them to get comfortable around me.

"Here, want to give them a treat?" I ask.

When her eyes light up, but she seems hesitant, I place one of the special treats in her hand. Then, flattening her hand, I place mine under hers and slowly move it toward Thunder.

"This guy is Thunder. Donna him because he sounds like thunder when he runs. He's been here almost ten years because he has Equine Metabolic Syndrome, so we monitor him closely." I tell her as Thunder licks her hand and takes the treat, causing her to giggle.

"What is Equine meta... whatever it was?" she asks.

"It's basically like diabetes in a horse."

"Oh no, should he have had that treat?" She looks concerned as she pets his head.

"No, he's fine. These treats are healthy so long as he doesn't eat half the bag," I say, as the next horse nudges his way in.

"This one here is Thunder's son Ruckus, named because he hates being in the barn and causes, well, a ruckus," I laugh and let Jenna feed him on her own.

We walk the fence line feeding horses and that's when Jenna notices a horse at the fence behind her.

"And who is this?"

He walks over and I don't move, waiting for the

horse to run like she always does from me, but she doesn't run from Jenna.

"This is Wild Lightning. She was the one hit by a car. The day you showed up here, she was the one I had been working on. One of the volunteers named her," I say. Then watch closely as Jenna walks up to the horse.

Wild Lightning has her head over the fence and brushes her nose over Jenna's belly.

"Do you think she can sense I'm pregnant?" Jenna asks, petting the horse.

When Jenna offers her a treat, Wild Lightning sniffs at it hesitantly at first before eating it.

"Yes, I think she knows you're pregnant. Animals are very intuitive like that. At this point she might even hear the baby's heartbeat," I tell Jenna.

While Wild Lightning is distracted, I take a step closer so I can reach Jenna quickly in the event it's needed. This horse is as wild as they come and hasn't let anyone near her. If she is near the fence and someone gets even closer than I am now, she will run off.

"Will she be able to be released?" Jenna asks as Wild Lightning nuzzles her belly again.

"I think so. She is healing nicely, but I'll be able to tell more in another week or two."

Eventually, another volunteer steps out of the barn, and Wild Lightning takes off. Jenna watches her go and I walk to Jenna's side. I'm in awe of how this horse acted with her. In my experience, animals, mostly horses and dogs, were some of the best judges of character.

"She is one of the true wild mustangs, and doesn't let anyone near her. In order to work on her, I had to tranquilizer her. So, how she was with you isn't her normal behavior. Just be careful around her and don't ever go into the field with her, okay?"

Jenna nods and we head back toward the front office to get going now that people are starting to show up. When Ruby sees us, I'm holding Jenna's hand and a smile lights up her face.

"Well now, don't you work fast? I just put that ad up!" Ruby says, looking smug.

"Oh, we aren't together." Jenna says, dropping my hand. I look over at her and frown.

Right then, it hits me hard. I wish we were together. Then I guide Jenna away from Ruby and to the conference room where Donna has set up all the eggs for the girls to stuff.

Luna, Emma, and Kinley are already there talking.

"Hey ladies, thank you for helping with this. Did Donna get you all set up?" I ask.

"Yep, we were just waiting on you to hand over Jenna," Luna jokes and the other join in.

"Okay, well, it's simple. One candy and one of the little horse erasers per egg. The red eggs over here are the peanut free ones to go with the candy next to them. The yellow eggs are lactose free candy. The rest can be mixed over there. When you are ready for lunch, let Donna know as she will be going into town for a few things and will grab some pizza or subs for y'all."

The girls take their seats and I turn to Jenna.

"You have your phone?" I check.

"Yep," she holds it up.

"Call or text if you need me, but stay in this building, okay? There will be a lot of people in and out today and I won't know all of them. Donna and Charles are here if you need anything too."

"I'll be fine. Go, I'm sure someone is looking for you by now."

As I leave, I try to focus on getting everything for the egg hunt set up. It's more than just a kid's event. It's also a fundraiser for the refuge so I'm always very hands on. Only today all I can think about is how Jenna told Ruby we aren't together.

By the time we get home that night, it's still on my mind. So on our way home, I bring it up.

"Hey, earlier when you told Ruby we aren't together?" I ask.

"Well, we aren't. I didn't want to mislead her," Jenna says, and I get where she is coming from.

"Well, what if we were? I know you want me. Last night, I heard you and fuck, it was so damn sexy," I moan. Then I curse because my cock is straining against my zipper. All day, until now, I'd managed to keep him under control.

Parking the truck in front of my cabin, I turn to face Jenna, whose face is a beautiful shade of pink now.

"It's nothing to be embarrassed about and nothing I didn't do myself as well." I tell her and watch her face get even pinker.

"What if we were together until you leave? Instead of fighting this for the next six weeks, we give in and scratch the itch for each other while you are here?"

## CHAPTER 7
## JENNA

HE LEADS me into the house, but the moment the door closes, he has me pressed against it and his lips on mine. We both moan at the contact that we have both been craving.

Knowing it wasn't just the alcohol messing with my brain and he really is a good kisser is something that will haunt me forever. Now that I'm sober, I know I have never been kissed like this.

I can feel his need and want in this kiss. I've never felt so desired from just a kiss that it has my body on fire. My knees weaken and every touch was like electricity throughout my body, making me ache with need.

His hands run up and down my sides before gripping my sides and hoisting me up. When I wrap my legs around his waist, I expect him to push me against the door, but he doesn't. Instead, he heads toward the dining room, setting me on the large solid table.

Only then does he break the kiss. His eyes lock with mine as he reaches up and runs a finger over my bottom lip, then trails it down my neck, over my collar bone before tracing the neckline of my sweater which shows a hint of cleavage. His breathing picks up, matching mine.

"You are so damn beautiful," he whispers. Then he places both hands on my hips and leans in for a quick kiss. A much too short one before pulling off my sweater and his. Both landing on the floor beside him.

I'm wearing my favorite pale pink lace bra, but it's too small and my boobs are spilling out of them.

"These have gotten bigger," he says, gently cupping them.

"Pregnancy side effect," I whisper.

"One I definitely like."

He pulls the cups down and sucks on one of my nipples. When he glides his tongue round the hard peak that forms, I can't stop how vocal I am. Switching to my other nipple, he pinches it slightly, causing a shiver throughout my body.

"They are sensitive too," he smiles, keeping his eyes on them

Finally, he removes my bra and adds it to the growing pile of clothes on the floor. Then he takes his time looking at me, which makes my nipples harden to a point and my core tighten.

His eyes run over me, and he smiles before shaking his head and starts to remove his pants. I only get a second to admire him in all his muscled, beautiful, naked glory before he's standing between my legs again, pulling my pants off. Then he slowly removes my matching pink lace panties, causing me to get even wetter.

When we are both naked, time seems to stop for just a moment. His hands rest on my stomach and in his eyes are delight and amazement at my small baby bump. If I didn't know this was just a fling, I'd say it's a look of love.

Taking his time, he kisses me with gentleness, but hot desire. Then he pulls me to the edge of the table, pulling my legs wide. In the next breath, his cock is at my opening. He gently lies me down on the table before slowly sliding inside of me.

I moan, because this is exactly what I have needed. Him filling me, the delicious stretch, and the way he hits that perfect spot inside of me no one has touched before. Add in being extra sensitive from being pregnant and it's sensory overload. It doesn't take long until I'm right at the edge.

"You felt good before, but fuck, you feel even better now and I don't know how it's possible." He groans with each glide in and out of me.

"Asher… I," I can't even form a full sentence, but he still understands.

"It's okay baby, I got you. Come for me."

That little bit of permission has me exploding and convulsing. Asher follows me over before collapsing on top of me. It was only a moment before he stood and scooped me up, carrying me to the bedroom for round two.

AFTER ANOTHER ROUND OF LOVEMAKING, we ended up in my bed, lying there together. My head was on his shoulder and he was playing with my hair with one hand and his other was propped up behind his head.

We are in this comfortable bubble of the aftereffects of amazing sex. But there is something in the back of my head saying it wasn't just sex. This was more, even if we are ignoring it.

"Why did you want to be a nurse?" he asks.

"Well, my grandma was a nurse, and she always talked about how much she loved helping people. Then when my sister was little, she got really sick, and we spent a lot of time in the hospital, which was hard on me. Even though I knew she was ill, I didn't fully grasp what was going on. The nurses were there to help her and me. As I got older and understood more, it just stuck with me."

When it's quiet like and I snuggle even closer to him, I can hear his heartbeat and every breath he takes.

"How did you start with the Mustang Refuge?" I ask him.

"Well, I was a large animal vet on the rodeo circuit. You

know that. During the season, I didn't have a home base and was living out of my truck and trailer. That gets old fast. One thing I knew was that I wanted to settle down, but had no idea where. While on the PBR rodeo circuit, we did a rodeo in Billings. A few days later, there was another rodeo just outside Whitefish. But the vet was out sick and they asked me to fill in. I agreed and heard some people talking about the mustang refuge going up for sale. At the time, the vet who was doing the rodeo owned it."

Before continuing, he turns and kisses the top of my head.

"I felt this urge to take a look at it. So the day after the rodeo, I did. The guy gave me a tour and the entire time, my mind was whirling about how I could make this work. Though I knew nothing about the town other than what the guys had told me at the rodeo the day before. When they told me that this cabin came with it because it was on the back end of the property, I was sold. A business, a way to help people, and a place to live all in one sale. It was perfect. My first week here, Ruby introduced me to Jackson and he kind of took me under his wing. Now I couldn't be happier about the choice that I've made."

His story definitely sounds like one of those instances where everything just came together. I always had this theory that if you were working towards something and it all came together so organically, you had to be on the right track. Which meant you were doing what you were supposed to be doing. Unfortunately, my move to Billings has been anything but easy, and I have to wonder if I still believe that if it's easy, it's the right thing. Because that would mean that the opposite is also true. If something is causing one problem after another like this move to Billings, then maybe it's not the right thing to do.

Though, I would never admit that out loud because I can't give up on my career. I need to have a way to support this child and this raise with the promotion is the best way to do it. I can't even count how many times growing up I heard my mother complaining about how much she wished she had not given up her career for my father.

My mom was a successful real estate broker, which is how my parents met. But when she got pregnant with me, he asked her to stay home to take care of me. At first it was just for a year or two until I could go to school, but about the time I was going into preschool, she wound up pregnant with my sister. Then the clock started all over again.

Since my sister was so sick, she never did go to preschool. By the time my mom was ready to go back to work, my sister was in second grade. Unfortunately, Mom had been out of the workforce for way too long and she'd have to go back to school to get her license again. There just wasn't time anymore, so she decided to be a stay at home with me and my sister. My father was more than happy to let her do it.

"Well, I'll let you get some sleep. Tomorrow is a big day with the Easter Egg Hunt and getting you settled here before you have to go to work ," he says. Standing in all his naked glory, he walks to the door before turning around to look at me, catching me staring at his firm and sculpted butt.

Even though I quickly jerk my eyes up to his face, he's already smirking because I've been caught.

"Get some sleep, sweetheart, but let me know if you need anything." He turns, closing the door behind him, leaving me there.

He's doing exactly what we agreed on, satisfying each other's needs, but not anything more.

So why does this room feel so empty now? Why does the idea of sleeping alone not appeal to me?

## CHAPTER 8
## ASHER

THIS YEAR'S Easter egg hunt is even bigger than last year. The first year of the egg hunt, it was pretty small, with just the families of the people that worked and volunteered here. Some of the local families who Jackson and Miles were able to drum up took part.

Each year since it's been growing. People love coming out and spending time with the mustangs while they hunt for eggs. Not only do they have a great time, but the money that they spend helps the horses who are here. Now we have people coming from as far as several towns away and for the last few years, people from Billings have heard about and come for the event.

Taking a walk around, I make sure everything is in order, and that nobody needs anything. Emma, Luna, Kinley, and Jenna are all working the face painting booth and have a line of kids excited to get their faces done. The tents that they're using are heated, which all of us guys insisted on for our girls.

Since none of the girls are super skilled artists, we made sure there were other fun things for the kids. The tattoos we got were a huge hit. They would press them on and then add glitter and paint to really make them pop. Not surprisingly, the most popular tattoos seem to be the horse ones. Even though we feel for these poor parents who are going to go home and have glitter all over their house, we still include this event because the kids enjoy it.

"Hey girls doing, okay? Do you need anything?" I ask, looking at Jenna who, despite the line of kids, seems calm and relaxed.

"I'm good. I've been taking bathroom breaks as needed and that gives me a chance to refill my water. Ruby brought over some of the food to try out, so I have even eaten," she says.

When she answers my next few questions, it helps me to relax a bit, knowing that she's cared for by more than just me.

"Okay, well, if you need anything, I have my phone on me. Don't hesitate to call."

"Shoot Asher, we can take care of her. You can go, we're having fun." Luna waves me off pretending to be irritated, but there's a big smile on her face too.

Next I head to the Easter bunny tents where there's a long line of kids waiting to get their picture taken with the Easter Bunny. This year, the girls were able to sweet talk Mack into dressing up as the Easter Bunny. Mostly he said yes because he'd be able to have the costume on and no one would see his scars. But the icing on the cake for him was that the girls promised him all kinds of home-cooked meals.

Though he was reluctant to do it, he seems to be doing really well with the kids and Donna is right there to help him out as needed. Because the mask hides his face and scar, he is a lot more relaxed and almost enjoying himself.

Right now, we have some volunteers going over the field that we used for the Easter egg hunt this morning making sure all the eggs were picked up. Also, that no candy spilled out and that there's no debris on the field so that we can reuse it for the horses next week. They're also getting set up for the toddler egg hunt. We learned pretty early on to do a separate one for the toddlers so that they weren't fighting with bigger kids for the eggs.

Once the toddler event is ready and the toddlers are on the field, pretty much everything stops, so everyone gets ready to cheer them on. I love that kind of unity that we get from Mustang Mountain.

Standing beside me, Jenna is watching and I know that we're both thinking next year it could be our little one out there as well. Maybe not walking, but at least enjoying picking up Easter eggs.

"Next year we'll be out there on the field ourselves helping little Wilbur pick up Easter eggs," I say, picturing it all in my head.

"We are so not naming our son after the pig in *Charlotte's Web*," Jenna says, sounding completely horrified.

"Wilbur was my grandfather's name, and I've always wanted to name my son after him. He was pretty much the only male figure in my life growing up," I tell her with all seriousness.

Even though she doesn't protest my announcement, she also doesn't agree. I know now is not the time to talk about it. We don't even know if we're having a boy or a girl.

Know when to pick your battles and it is not it today. I want her to have a good day full of fun, so that she has great memories here at the refuge. Because bottom line, I want her to look forward to coming back, not dread it.

After the toddler egg hunt, I head over to grab myself some lunch. Because while I made sure Jenna has eaten, I still haven't. The food is in another heated tent and Lily is catering. Over the years, she has catered several of the events here and is now the only one to cater the Easter egg hunt because she's who everyone requests.

The only exception to that was last year. I forget what happened, but she wasn't available, so the town decided to do a potluck style, which turned out pretty good. But collectively I think they were all relieved when they found out Lily was going to be catering again this year.

What really catches my eye is that she's talking with Mack. Granted, he still has his Easter Bunny costume on, and for whatever reason, that seems to help him relax. She's laughing and I can tell from his body language that he is too.

But they also catch Ruby's attention. One thing I know is that he's not going to be thrilled to know that if Ruby even catches the hint of something between them. She will try to play matchmaker. Later I'll do the benefit of giving him a heads up.

As I stand there staring at all the families having fun, I'm realizing how easily Jenna has adjusted to my life. She's talking with families, giving directions and seamlessly fits into my life better than I ever thought a woman could. She's only been living with me for a couple days. How entangled will our lives be in six weeks?

## CHAPTER 9
## JENNA

**TODAY IS** the day that we find out whether our little baby is a boy or a girl and I'm so excited because. Asher is certain that it's a boy and I have a feeling that it's a girl. Emma, Luna and Kinley came over the other day and we did some of the old wives' tales to see what they said. A majority of them said, girl.

So, today is where we find out who was right.

With my appointments being in the afternoon, I came in and worked half a day, and I'm leaving now. Asher is supposed to meet me there. I guess one of the benefits of working in a doctor's office is they understand the amount of stress that I am currently under. Even though they're doing everything they can to make the transition from one of their offices to the other as smooth as possible. A move in general is still stressful when you're pregnant.

When I need to take these half days for things like

doctor's appointments, they've been very lenient and I am so grateful.

When I get to the doctor's office, I am there first, so I park and take my time walking in. After checking in, I sit down in the waiting room. While I'm waiting, I text Asher.

I don't get anything back, but I figure he's probably driving and almost here he doesn't want to bother trying to read a text message. It's one thing I noticed, he's a very safe driver.

When the nurse comes out and calls the other two ladies that were in the waiting room before me, I start to get nervous. He's always been early to these appointments. To the point that most of the time, he beats me here, even when I leave early. Then all the doubts I used to have as a kid start scrolling through my mind. I have to remind myself that he's not my dad.

Asher's proven that he's going to show up and be here for me. But my confidence dwindles when the nurse comes out and calls my name.

Following her to the back, I go through all the normal check-in procedures.

"The baby's dad should be here at any time. His name is Asher. Will you let him come on back?" I say, as she shows me to my room.

"Of course, sweetheart. All he has to do is check in at the counter."

Once she leaves and I am in the room alone, I take out my phone and call Asher. Hoping maybe it's just a traffic delay and I can ask the doctor to wait. The phone rings and he doesn't pick up. So I hang up. And try again, still nothing.

Just as I'm trying to get a handle on my emotions, flutters in my belly start. It's our little one moving around and trying to get my attention. It's like he or she is reminding me that I need to stay strong for them, and that is so much more important right now.

So, I take a deep breath, sit down on the exam table, and wait. The doctor must be behind because I wait for a little while. But then my phone rings, and I breathed a sigh of relief that I didn't realize I was holding.

"Hey, I'm here. Are you okay?" I ask answering the phone.

"Don't be mad, but I'm not going to be able to make it in time," his voice fills my ear. But instantly, I'm that sad, upset little girl whose dad didn't show up at her ballet recital. Or the scared teenager dealing with a broken arm, whose father couldn't even be bothered to pick up the phone.

"I don't care what your excuse is. This was important and it's our child," I say, trying not to let on how upset I am getting into my voice.

"Listen, I know and I would be there if I could. I just couldn't avoid this. Please let me explain."

"I really don't care what your excuse is," I tell him, hanging up the phone.

My dad would say the same thing. It was unavoidable and he couldn't get to me in time, or it was important for him to keep his job. For this client who just came out of nowhere. And for a while, I believed him. But the older I got, the more I could tell there was always something more important. Another woman, or maybe it was just the high of chasing the job, I don't know. But his kids never made his priority list.

There's a knock on the door and my doctor steps in. She does her normal checks and then leads me down the hallway to the ultrasound room. The tech there is all smiles, and I realized this should be one of the happiest moments of my life.

Screw Asher, and whatever his excuses. I'm not going to let him rob me of enjoying this.

After I get situated on the table, the technician gets the machine all ready to go.

"All right. Let's get these measurements. Now, do you want to know if it's a boy or a girl?" She asks, as she squirts some cold gel onto my belly.

"Yes, I'd like to know. I think it's a girl, though," I tell her with a smile on my face.

When she moves the wand over my belly, grainy black and white images popped up on the screen. Before I know it, the shape of a little baby fills the screen. You can see his or her skull. The little body is curled up in there perfectly.

The technician is busy taking measurements, photos, and doing whatever. As she does what she is supposed to do, I stare at the screen in complete awe. At one point, she flips the heartbeat on, and you can hear the movement in the heartbeat that matches along with the screen.

"All right, it looks like right here. We have a baby boy." She shows the picture that clearly outlines that there is a penis growing inside of me.

A little baby boy. It looks like Asher was right. Then it hits me. That I don't want this child to grow up, like I did with my dad, full of broken promises and false hopes. I always knew it but knowing it's a baby boy, and seeing it on the screen it just it's so much harder.

I don't want to continue to live my life like that either. One thing I know is I am perfectly strong enough to do this on my own.

Why had I let myself start to dream and hope of a life where Asher was involved? Maybe where we would be able to work things out and became one big happy family.

He had some girl living in his house. It was easy access to sex, so why not? He's just a guy and that's what their driving force is. I still let myself fall for him, anyway.

Just like my dad, he's not going to take care of his responsibilities.

The ultrasound tech prints out a ton of pictures and hands me a stack of them.

"I printed out some extras for you to give to Dad or Grandma and Grandpa. Whoever you would like." She gives me a wink, but I just keep the smile on my face. It's not her fault that she has no idea what's going on or that the baby's father didn't show up. And I will not take it out on her.

Checking out, I make my next appointment without even giving a second thought to Asher and his schedule, or what's going on. I'm hoping by the time that I'm due for this appointment, I will be in Billings anyway, and I will just be rescheduling it with my new doctor.

Once in my car, I drive a few blocks down to one of my favorite little city parks. After finding a parking space, I walk along one of the trails to a bench that overlooks a small lake. While I sit there trying to decide what I'm going to do, I realize at some point I have to go back to Asher's. If for no other reason than to get my stuff.

As I'm trying to figure out where I'm going to stay, my phone rings. It's the landlord for the place I rented in Billings.

He tells me that the tenants that were in there moved out earlier than he expected and he has gotten the place clean. The last thing is to have the carpets shampooed which will be done tomorrow and I can move in any time after that if I would like. He wouldn't even charge me the extra time on my lease because of the hassle.

It was like a message on the direction I'm supposed to go here. I am trying to figure out where to go or stay and now my apartment is ready.

Proving once again, the easy path points the way.

Without hesitation, I head back to Asher's house and I'm beyond thankful that he is not there when I arrive. Part of me wonders if he's going to try to show up at the doctor's office, thinking I'm still there waiting for him.

Thankfully, I didn't take most of my things out of the boxes. And I have an SUV. So I fold all the seats flat and start loading up all the boxes. They take up all the space in my car and I start to wonder how I'm going to get my clothes in.

My clothes were in a box of their own and I realize I can just shove the clothes in wherever they will fit. They don't have to go in a box. So, that's what I do. Any nook and cranny gets filled with clothes. I won't be able to see out of my rearview mirror, but at least everything will be in my car.

I do the same with my bathroom things, shove them in wherever there's room.

Then I go to Asher's office and that's when I see the car seats that he bought. For a moment I pause, thinking that's the man that bought those two car seats. These car seats seem to tell a different story than the man who would miss one of the most important doctor's appointments during this pregnancy,

Would he have the same excuse during the birth that he would miss that, too?

I don't think I can stand to be around and find out.

Grabbing a piece of paper and a pen that I came in here for, I go to the dining room table to quickly write out a letter.

For now, I need to do this for myself to give me a sense of closure on all this. But to say what? Not wanting to leave any open doors, but I know I don't want to say anything in person.

I don't want him to think that we can just go back to where things were, either.

All the way back to the cabin, I've been working on what I want to say. So the words just fly. From my mind to my hand and onto the paper.

When I'm done, I read the letter. And it sounds exactly like I'd like it too. So I set it in the pen on the table.

Then I take his house key off my key ring and place it on top.

After giving the house one last look, I turn around and walk out the door, locking it behind me.

## CHAPTER 10
## ASHER

I KNOW Jenna is mad at me and she has every right because it was such a special appointment. If I can just get her to listen to me, then I can explain I was on my way. On the two-lane county road, there was a car in front of me that swerved, trying to avoid an animal that darted into the road. The car went off the road, hit the ditch, flipped into the air and came crashing down.

Since I was the only other car on the road, I flew into action. While calling 911 and giving them the details, I raced to aid the people inside.

Clearly, it was a family, tourists taking a scenic drive. There was a husband, his wife and their kid who thankfully will all be okay. But, I couldn't just leave them there. I had to wait until help arrived and then I had to answer questions with the police to let them know what happened.

By the time I was able to leave, I didn't think there was any point in trying to make the doctor's appointment. It took me so long that she was probably already at my cabin. So, I came straight home.

But now that I sit here, I can see that her car isn't here. I wonder if maybe she stopped along the way. Though I didn't see her car pass by me on the road. But I doubt she would have come that way.

What kills me is if it hadn't been for the accident, I would have been at the doctor's appointment with plenty of time. Probably even before she was. And now she's mad at me and I'm sure it's going to take some effort and convincing to get her back.

My guess is she's probably stewing and talking to her sister as we speak.

Going inside, I figure I can at least get dinner going. That way, I can make sure that she's eaten by the time she gets home. As I head to the kitchen, the piece of paper on the table catches my eye.

When I left this morning, I cleaned off the table after breakfast. So I know it wasn't there, nor did I leave it there. Then I spot my house key and a letter from Jenna, proving she's been here and gone. Not bothering to even read the letter, I just know. Walking down to her bedroom, I find all of her stuff gone.

My heart sinks and suddenly I feel nauseous. Then, as my knees give out from underneath me, I slide down the wall to the floor. And with shaky hands, I read the letter.

## ASHER,

These past couple weeks, I have been fooling myself that we could make this work between us and be more than what they've been.

Today proved that you have other priorities that are not me and this baby.

And I know how this story goes. I do not want my child constantly disappointed because their dad never shows up.

As I told you from the beginning and I meant it, I am perfectly capable of raising this baby on my own and am fully planning to do just that. I would rather you not be in the baby's life than to be there and constantly disappointing them, because you're simply not there when they need you.

This letter is to inform you that I don't want anything from you. Not even any child support or help from you. Though you need to know that you have a child, and if you want to visit them, I won't stop you. But don't make plans and cancel. That's the one thing I will not tolerate.

If you're not sure that you can keep plans, it would almost be better for your visit to be a surprise versus actually making plans you don't know if you'll be able to keep.

Thank you for opening your house to me.

And thank your friends for inviting me into their circle for a brief time.

The landlord in Billings called and my apartment there is ready early. So I'm going to go there and get it all sorted out.

It was just perfect timing.

Once again, thank you again for everything, Jenna

READING this letter over and over, I'm confused and shocked. I can't help feeling like it's such a drastic leap from me missing the appointment to her up and leaving.

Not able to wrap my head around it, I pull out my phone and give her a call.

And just like I expected, it goes right to voicemail. Then I leave a message explaining about the car crash, including every detail that I can cram into it. All the while praying to God that she will listen to it and understand. Praying with urgency that we can work this out.

Then I call back again, leaving a second voicemail.

I tell her that I want to be part of both of their lives. Also that she wasn't fooling herself because I too was imagining what our life could be like these past couple weeks and how badly I want her. I want our baby here, and growing up here. Most of all, I want what we've had, but I want even more.

Then I sit there and wait.

I wait, praying against hope that she will call me back.

That we can talk about this.

That there's a chance for us after all.

When my phone rings, I scramble so fast to answer it. I don't even check the caller ID.

"Jenna, please let me explain," I say, but it's Ford's voice that greets me instead.

"WELL, I guess that answers whether you will be joining us tonight or not. What happened?"

I completely forgot that the couple's dinner was tonight. We were supposed to join Emma and Jackson, Ford and Luna, and Miles and Kinley for dinner.

"No, we won't be making it. The doctor's appointment was today and on the way, a car crashed in front of me. It swerved off the road and flipped. The accident was horrible. Of course, I had to stop and help them. It was a family with a young kid in the car. The entire process of helping them and making sure medical help got there took a lot of time. Then I had to give my statement to the authorities. I missed the appointment, but Jenna wouldn't let me explain. She was very upset that I didn't show up. And when I came home, she had packed her stuff and left and I have not talked to her," I pour my heart out. Then I hang up and go into the kitchen.

I pour myself a drink down it and then pour another one. Everything hurt, thinking that I had her here and I was so close to having everything that I wanted. Then in one afternoon with something that was completely unavoidable, I've lost everything.

The woman that I now know I am head over heels in love with. Not just the mother of my child, but I in love my child.

I don't know what to do. All I know is it hurts.

It hurts more than the time that I was kicked by that bull in Phoenix.

It hurts more than the time that the horse at the Las Vegas Rodeo stomped on my foot, breaking more bones than I can count.

My entire body feels like that pain, only magnified.

Grabbing the bottle, I head into the living room, collapsing on the couch and think.

If can't get her to listen about what happened, how the hell am I going to win her back?

I don't know how long I sit on that couch or how many drinks in I am, but next thing I know, Jensen and his brother Jonas are walking through the front door. They are followed by Owen and Ace.

"Ford called us and told us what happened. He said it was probably not a good idea for you to be alone," Jensen says, walking over and plucking the bottle out of my hand.

They seem to understand that I don't want to talk about it because we start discussing things going on in town, the horses, and Ruby. That is, until all the couples show up after their dinner.

Once again, I relay what happened for the girls, who want much more detailed information than Ford got from me.

"It was a very important appointment and I guarantee you her hormones are running strong. Once she comes around and comes down, and listens to your voicemail, I think she'll change her mind," Emma says,

"I'm not so sure," I say.

Then I show them the letter and everyone reads it as it gets passed around.

Once Luna reads it, she gets up and comes to sit down next to me.

"You know, we've had a lot of time to talk over the last couple weeks, and one thing that I learned about Jenna is that she didn't really have it easy growing up," Luna says.

"I know about her sister being sick," I say, assuming that's where she's going.

"Well, that was really only part of it. Her dad, while married to her mom, he was just never around. He didn't do family dinners and was never there when she needed him.

From what I understand, he was never a parent that was at the dance recitals or school plays or sports events. He wasn't even at her high school graduation. He never showed up, even when he always promised to, and she would get her hopes up time and time again.

That type of childhood trauma really does follow someone, and now she's getting ready to have her own child. And the last thing she wants is for her child to experience the same type of hurt that she did.

"Of course, she is struggling with that because this was not how she had planned to have a family." Luna says.

"You absolutely had a legitimate reason for not being there today. If it wasn't for all the crazy hormones, she would probably completely understand. But hormones during pregnancy make women do crazy things. In our brains, the most rational decisions just don't make sense to us.

"So what it sounds like is she's having all these doubts. Then the first time you go and are not where you said you would be, she's instantly equating that to her dad," Kinley says, and Luna agrees.

"Why didn't she tell me all of this?" I ask, thinking out loud.

"Because this isn't stuff you talk about to someone that you're just sleeping with. Or someone that you have an arrangement for just sex," Luna says, giving me a pointed look.

# CHAPTER 11
# JENNA

MY SISTER and I are out for dinner, taking a break from all the moving. She and her husband, my new brother-in-law, have been troopers about helping me get moved from Whitefish to Billings.

Yesterday morning, we were able to get the keys and move everything into the house. Now, they're staying for a couple days to help me unpack.

After visiting a baby store this morning, we got the crib and a dresser for the baby. Thankfully, my brother-in-law is at the house, putting them together. While he was doing that, he insisted we go to lunch, so I wasn't tempted to help. His exact words.

"All right, it's just us. Now you're going to have to tell me what is going on. You look like someone stole your puppy and broke your favorite toy," my sister says. She doesn't waste a minute and asks as soon as our butts are in the chair at the restaurant.

Until now, all my sister knows is that my place

became available early, and that I was taking advantage of the opportunity to get in right away. She never questioned it because she didn't have a reason why she should. So, under her probing stare, I break down and let it all out.

"We had the ultrasound the other day to find out if it was a boy or a girl and he didn't even show up. We've been living together for a couple weeks and things had changed. I was starting to believe he truly wanted to be around, not just for the kid, but for me. At that point, I thought maybe there was something more to our relationship. Then he didn't even bother to show up for one of the biggest appointments of the pregnancy."

My sister is younger than me, and her being sick, she doesn't quite remember everything with our dad the way I do. But it seemed like after that he was around even less than he was before.

After asking Mom about it, I remember she said that there were a lot of hospital bills from my sister's care, and that he was working overtime to help pay them off. For a long time, I believed her. But now I'm not so sure. My dad had a good job with great health insurance.

"Did you talk to Asher? What was his reasoning?"

Huffing, I roll my eyes, pulling up his voicemail and play it for my sister.

"What's this second voicemail from him?" she plays it as well.

"Okay, this cannot be the only thing that drove you

to essentially run away because this is a very legitimate reason for missing that appointment and you know it."

"He was coming on too strong. First, he is going to buy a townhouse in Billings so that he could be there with our kid on the weekends. Then he had already bought top of the line car seats for each of our cars for the baby and kept making all these plans. He wanted me to be more in his life. While I was there with him, we had an arrangement. It was just a sex to scratch an itch, but I let myself believe that it could be more. Then he wasn't there for our child's biggest appointment. Just like..." I can't bring myself to finish the rest of the sentence, but of course, my sister has been hanging on to every word.

"Just like, who?" She narrows her eyes at me and I know that she already knows who I'm about to say, but she's going to make me say it anyway.

"Just like Dad."

Saying those words brings back so many memories that I would rather keep locked away.

"Do you like him?" my sister asks,

"No, no, he's all wrong for me."

"How is he all wrong for you?"

"Come on, Haley. He's a veterinarian and I'm allergic to cats. No way I can be with a vet. I can't even stand to be around one of the basic animals they treat."

"First of all, you can take medication for your allergies and be fine. Second of all, he doesn't treat cats, he treats horses and cows and bears and deer. Animals that are as large as you. If I remember correctly, there's a vet in town that treats pets like dogs, cats and hamsters or other smaller animals. And it's not him."

"Well, what about his absolutely crazy schedule? If he gets a call about an injured animal, he drops everything to be there. And then misses important things like this doctor's appointment."

"Come on Jenna, he didn't miss that appointment because he dropped everything to rescue an animal. He missed that appointment because a family with a little kid was in a car accident right in front of him. Then he did what any decent human being would do, and he helped them and made sure that they were okay.

"With the little bit that I know about him, I'm willing to bet that if he had gotten a call for an animal and he had your doctor's appointment he was going to, he would have called someone else to do it.

As for him being like Dad, I want you to know that Dad had a big effect on me, too. The difference is I've been talking to a therapist about it. Because it affected my dating relationships, and I knew there was someone special out there for me. When I met my husband, I knew he was the one."

I love the way she goes out of her way to call him her husband and smiles every time that she does. It's so cute and I'm really happy for her. I hope to find that level of happiness one day.

"One thing I learned in therapy is that some people just don't have the ability and mentality to be a parent. And that's how it was with Dad. He was not made to be a parent. But I also know to this day, he still loves our mother fiercely. He would give her anything that she wanted and what she wanted was a family and kids. There's no telling what their agreement was. But they were happy.

"Dad got to chase his career. Mom got her family, and a husband that supported her. And for the record, my room was next door to theirs and they had a lot of sex while I was growing up. So, whatever their marriage was, it worked for them. That's all that matters.

"There are guys out there that can't wait to be a father. All they want is a family. Dad just wasn't that guy. Don't let him dictate your future." She pauses to take a sip of water.

Before I can respond, she continues. "Remember, Asher was there for everything else. He missed one thing. Don't write him off because of one incident. Especially for something that he stopped to do and what so many people wouldn't. Most people would have called 911 and kept going. But he stopped to check on them and stayed to pull the people out of that car.

"Can you imagine how scared those parents were for their kid in the backseat? How scared that child might have been? You're about to be a parent. Now, Jenna think about. If it had been you, would you have wanted someone to stop and help you and make sure that you were okay and waited until the paramedics got there? What would you rather? Someone who simply called 911 and left you to worry about your kids by yourself, or someone who stopped and helped?"

Dammit, of course, she's right. Even if my stubborn pregnancy hormones don't want me to admit it to her right now.

"Besides, the biggest question is, how does he make you feel?"

I can't stop the smile from spreading across my face if I tried.

"You don't have to answer me. That smile says it all," my sister says,

As mad as I am, he still gives me butterflies in my belly when I think of our time together. Remembering him still makes me smile. It's a very confusing feeling.

After dinner, I drop her back off at my house and head to this beautiful park that overlooks the city right by the airport. Stopping there, I watch the sunset and let myself think and remember.

As beautiful as this park is, it's nothing compared to the views from Mustang Mountain.

## CHAPTER 12
## ASHER

AFTER MY NIGHT of drinking with the guys, the killer hangover the next morning, and Hades howling outside my window, I'm guessing to tell me what an idiot I am, I get my ass in gear.

What Luna had to say about Jenna and her dad made me realize she's going to need some extra reassurance. I'm just the man who is going to give it to her.

I took the rest of the day to get a few things in order and today, I made the drive into Billings later than I had planned.

Which is way later than when I wanted to get to her new place. She was already out to dinner with her sister. But her brother-in-law offered to call them, but I told him no and that I'd wait. They probably need to talk and decompress anyway, and I didn't want to ruin it. Plus, she needs to eat.

So, I'm sitting on the front steps of her apartment

waiting for her to get back when her sister comes walking up.

"What took you so long to get here?" she asks, sitting down beside me.

What I finally ended up doing was texting her for Jenna's address here in Billings. Thankfully, she's been on my side.

"In order to prove that I mean what I say, I had to get a few things. Where is she?" I ask.

"We had a pretty deep conversation at dinner, so she went up to Swords Park to watch the sunset and to think."

Pulling out my phone, I look for the park.

"The one by the airport?" I ask just to be sure.

"Yep, that's the one. Good luck. You're going to need it."

After giving me a hug, she goes inside and I leave for the park. In all honesty, I'll take any luck I can get.

When I arrive at the park, I can see why she chose to come here. It's beautiful and overlooks the city. Not only is it breathtaking, but you get the views of the airplanes flying in.

It takes me a minute to find her car and thankfully, she's inside of it, which makes getting to her to talk easier. Pulling in beside her, I'm careful not to block her view. Then I get out, knocking on her window. She doesn't seem startled, which means she probably saw me pull up.

Our eyes lock as I wait for her to roll down the

window. Or flip me the bird and tell me to go away or start screaming at me. Anything at all.

Finally, she tilts her head towards the passenger side and I hear locks pop up. When I get in, her car smells of her and it instantly makes my heart ache to have her close. Yet there's so much distance between us and it instantly makes my heart ache to have her so close but so much distance between us.

"HOW DID YOU FIND ME?" she asks.

"Your sister told me you'd be here. Why didn't you tell me about your father?"

She just shrugs her shoulder and I know that this is a hard topic for her.

"I completely understand the need and the desire to protect our child from ever being hurt. The thought of you being here in Billings and me not being with my child every day kills me. I don't want to miss anything. Not the first steps, nor the first words, or the first smile. Every moment I want to be a part of their lives. I don't want to miss games or dance recitals or graduations, nothing.

I also know I can sit here and spout that off. All day long. But it's not going to mean anything until you give me a chance to prove it. But don't underestimate me, Jenna. I will prove it."

By now, the sun is starting to set and lighting up the city of Billings with brilliant colors.

"Come on. Let's go sit at that bench over there and get some fresh air," I tell her.

Once we're seated and enjoying the view, I tell her what I've done. "In order to spend more time with you two, I've hired more help at the Refuge. But I can't promise that I won't be late to some things. If I have an emergency call, I never know how those calls will go. Sometimes they can take me thirty minutes and sometimes they can take me three hours. But just know that I will be doing my best to be there."

"Asher, I don't need you to promise. I just need you to understand that my pregnancy hormones have been making me a bit crazy. After talking with my sister at dinner, I have come to realize that you're not like my dad. I don't want our son to ever have that disappointment or heartbreak."

At her words, my heart stops for a moment.

"It's a boy? We're having a boy?" I ask, needing to make sure I heard her correctly.

Smiling, she says, "I have ultrasound photos in my purse."

I pull her in for a hug and she snuggles into me. Just like she would melt into me like she used to do when we would cuddle in bed.

Kissing the top of her head, I enjoy having her by my side, and I'm not willing to let her go just yet. While I keep one arm around her, I reach into my pocket and pull out the house key, the one that she left, along with the note on the dining room table. Then I hold it out for her.

"All right. I'm going to take my shot here because I don't want there to ever be a question about whether I want you. First off, I really want you to move back in with me permanently. Both you and our son I want living with me. Also, the doctor's office in town has an available nurse position. While it's not the promotion that you came here for, I think it would be perfect for you. Not to mention that you'd be great in that role. You'd get to know everyone in town and make a difference in Mustang Mountain. Since you'd know everyone sooner or later, you could really be able to make a change and help families. It will be more one on one than here in Billings.

But even if you decide not to move in permanently and take the job. I'd like for you to have a key so that you can come visit anytime you want. No notice required."

"Luna had sent me a text with the job opening earlier today," Jenna says. "After the talk with my sister, I sent in my resume before I even left the parking lot of the restaurant. On the way here, I got a phone call. The day after tomorrow, I have an interview at the doctor's office in Mustang Mountain," she continues with a smile on her face.

It takes a minute for what that means to sink in. Before I even showed up, she was making plans to come back to me!

"I love you, Jenna, and our son so much. Every day I plan to spend trying to convince you to agree to marry me. So I'm putting you on notice. You take as long as you need to say yes. Because once you make that commitment, you are mine. I need you to understand that."

"Well, it's not going to take very much convincing," she says with a shy smile.

Once again, my heart once starts racing.

I've taken several chances today and they've paid off. What the hell is one more? I pull out the ring that's been in my pocket for a solid week now and drop to one knee in front of her.

"The day of the ultrasound, that accident screwed up more than one thing. By then, I realized I was madly in love with you and didn't want you to leave. Nor did I want you to take this job in Billings. I wanted you to stay. Right after the ultrasound, I was going to ask you to marry me, but I didn't get the chance. So, I'm going to ask you now. That night of your sister's bachelorette party, there was a connection between us. It was strong and intense, unlike anything I have ever felt before.

Falling asleep that night, I had plans for us the next day, but you were gone. For a while, I thought I would never see you again, but the universe seems to have had other plans. I want to be your husband and I want to be this baby's father. I want to coach little league and help you plan birthday parties. Hell, I'm even up for the three a.m. feedings and diaper changes. As long as you're by my side through it all. I know that marriage isn't going to be easy. Especially since we're starting it off with a kid. But I do know that I want to spend every day fighting for you and for us, and for our family.

Because the love that I feel for you is the kind of love that many don't find in a lifetime. But we were lucky enough to find on a one-night stand. Will you marry me? "

At this point, she's in tears and all she can do is nod.

"Yes." She gasps between tears and I slide the ring on her finger.

Then she gulps and sits back down.

"What's wrong? Are you okay?" I ask, worried about her.

She pulls me to the bench next to her and takes my hand, placing it on her belly. A moment later, our son kicks my hand and my eyes shoot up to her. It's such a faint little kick, but he's there and involved in the moment we really start our family.

Our story is just beginning. And I can't wait to get her back to Mustang Mountain. And get started on it.

# EPILOGUE
## MACK

I DIDN'T HAVE time to go all the way into town this afternoon to meet Ruby, but somehow I could never say no to her. None of the guys who lived on Mustang Mountain could. She might be annoying as hell sometimes and stick her nose into places where it definitely didn't belong, but she was as much a part of Mustang Mountain as the landscape itself.

Before I took off, I needed to check on my new hire. Caden had only been working with me for a few weeks, but seemed to have a good handle on what needed to be done. I ducked into one of the outbuildings on my property where I kenneled some of the sled dogs, who were just about ready for breeding. My team was already behind schedule this spring. If we didn't get these females bred soon, we might as well forget about it this season.

"Hey, boss." Caden looked up as I entered. He was my buddy Shaw's younger brother, and I'd taken him under my wing in an effort to keep him out of trouble. "I think you need to take a look at Persephone before we match her up with Triton."

"What makes you think that?" Persephone was only three years old, but she'd been one of my best sled dogs over the winter. Even a mention that there might be something wrong with her made my stomach roll.

"It's nothing bad. She's just acting a little funny," Caden said.

"It will have to wait. I've got to run into town for a while, and I'm not sure when I'll be back. You think you can finish up around here on your own this afternoon?"

"Yeah, I can do that." Caden's chest puffed out a bit.

The kid had been doing a good job and deserved to take on some additional responsibilities. He reminded me of one of the recruits I'd trained back when I worked as a firefighter in Texas. I hadn't thought about my time there in a while. There was no use since I couldn't go back and change the past. I pushed the memories that threatened away and refocused on Caden.

"Good. Everything that needs to be done is on the list. Make sure you lock up the office when you leave and keep an eye out for Hades." The big wolf was more town mascot than wild animal, but he could tell it was breeding season, and I'd caught him sniffing around a lot more than usual over the past couple of weeks.

"Will do. Don't worry about a thing. I've got it all under control." Caden gave me a cocky grin.

I shook my head before I walked out the door, hoping like hell I hadn't misplaced my trust in him. I'd done that with someone else once, and it had almost cost me everything.

A HALF HOUR LATER, I pulled my baseball cap down low and pushed through the doors of the Nelson Mercantile. Ruby didn't say exactly what she needed, only that it had to do with some event she wanted to pull together at the last minute that would involve my dogs.

I'd only been living in Mustang Mountain for a couple of years, but I'd already learned that when Ruby got a wild hair up her ass, it was better to get involved at the start. Otherwise, she'd make her own plans and expect everyone else to rearrange their lives to conform to her wishes.

I lifted a hand and waved at her husband, Orville, who was working behind the front counter. He was also the mayor, but folks around here didn't bother to put on airs. Ruby stood at the back of the store, one hand gripping a carafe of coffee and the other already reaching for a mug.

"Hey, Mack. Thanks for stopping by." She set the mug down in front of me and filled it with the strong-smelling brew.

"It didn't seem like I had much of a choice," I said,

only halfway joking. "What's so important that it couldn't wait a few days?"

She put the carafe back on the warmer and leaned against the counter. "You're a few minutes early. I'd rather wait until everyone's here to go over the details, so I only have to do it once."

"What are you talking about? Who else is coming?" My jaw immediately clenched. I hated being caught off guard. She hadn't said anything about this being a group project.

"Well, we can't very well have an event without refreshments." Ruby smiled at someone behind me. "Here she comes now."

I knew what she was up to before I turned around. Damn her for setting herself up to be some self-appointed Cupid.

Ruby patted a spot on the counter to my left. "Lily, I'm so glad you could make it. Come sit down next to Mack so I can fill the two of you in on what I have in mind."

I turned slightly, just far enough to get a good look at the woman I hadn't been able to get out of my mind. We met last month at the Easter egg hunt my MC club had put on. Lily was everything I'd ever wanted in a woman. She ran her own successful catering business and had a need to succeed that rivaled my own. Pair that with glossy black hair reaching all the way down her back to skim the top of her heart-shaped ass, and big blue eyes rimmed with full, dark lashes, and I'd fallen for her in the space of a single afternoon.

"Any chance you've got a cup of coffee for me, Ruby?" She slid onto the stool next to me and held out her hand. "Mack, it's good to see you again. Or maybe I should say it's good to finally see you, since you were wearing a bunny suit the first time we met."

Just hearing her voice sent heat racing through my veins. If I took her hand, I might not be able to ever tear myself away. Why had Ruby put me in an impossible situation? I kept my head turned so Lily couldn't see the right side of my face. The scars didn't bother me most of the time, but I didn't want to witness her reaction when she saw them for the first time.

"I don't want to be rude, but I just remembered I need to pick up an order at the bakery before they close." It was a lame excuse, but the best I could do under the circumstances. Pulling the collar of my jacket up to hide my cheeks, I glared at Ruby. "I'm sorry to run out on you both like this. I'll follow up with you tomorrow, Ruby."

Ruby's shoulders slumped in defeat. "I'm sure Orville would be happy to run over and get that for you, Mack."

I was already halfway to the door and had no intention of turning around. "I'll call you in the morning," I tossed over my shoulder before I escaped through the front door.

The cool spring air hit my face as I stepped out onto the sidewalk, and I gulped in a huge breath. I'd managed to avoid Lily for the past few weeks, but I wouldn't be able to keep it up forever, especially if Ruby was involved.

She got lucky when Jackson, Ford, Miles, and Asher fell in love, and didn't see anything wrong with taking the credit. If she thought she could make me into the next Mustang Mountain bachelor, she was dead wrong. She might think a woman like Lily would be able to see past my scars, but she had no idea exactly how deep they ran.

WANT MORE ASHER AND JENNA? **Sign up for our newsletter** and get the free bonus scene here: subscribepage.io/oiM0N3

Make sure to grab Mack's story in **May is for Mack**. Then Jensen is up in **June is for Jensen!**

https://books2read.com/May-Mack
https://books2read.com/June-Jensen

If you want more on Jack from Whiskey River, make sure to check out the Mountain Men of Whiskey River starting with **Take Me To The River**.

https://books2read.com/TakeMeToTheRiver2

# MOUNTAIN MEN OF MUSTANG MOUNTAIN

*Welcome to Mustang Mountain where love runs as wild as the free-spirited horses who roam the hillsides. Framed by rivers, lakes, and breathtaking mountains, it's also the place the Mountain Men of Mustang Mountain call home. They might be rugged and reclusive, but they'll risk their hearts for the curvy girls they love.*

To learn more about the Mountain Men of Mustang Mountain, visit our website (https://www.matchofthemonthbooks.com/) join our newsletter here (http://subscribepage.io/MatchOfTheMonth) or follow our Patreon here (https://www.patreon.com/MatchOfTheMonth)

**January is for Jackson** - https://www.matchofthemonthbooks.com/January-Jackson

**February is for Ford** - https://www.matchofthemonthbooks.com/February-Ford

**March is for Miles** - https://www.matchofthemonthbooks.com/March-Miles

**April is for Asher** - https://www.matchofthemonthbooks.com/April-Asher

**May is for Mack** - https://www.matchofthemonthbooks.com/May-Mack

**June is for Jensen** - https://www.matchofthemonthbooks.com/June-Jensen

## ACKNOWLEDGMENTS

A huge, heartfelt thanks goes to everyone who's supported us in our writing, especially our HUSSIES of Mountain Men of Mustang Mountain patrons:

Jackie Ziegler

To learn more about the Mountain Men of Mustang Mountain on Patreon, visit us here: https://www.patreon.com/MatchOfTheMonth

## OTHER BOOKS BY KACI ROSE

**Oakside Military Heroes Series**

**Saving Noah** – Lexi and Noah

**Saving Easton** – Easton and Paisley

**Saving Teddy** – Teddy and Mia

**Saving Levi** – Levi and Mandy

**Saving Gavin** – Gavin and Lauren

**Saving Logan** – Logan and Faith

**Saving Ethan** – Bri and Ethan

**Saving Zane** — Zane

**Mountain Men of Whiskey River**

**Take Me To The River** – Axel and Emelie

**Take Me To The Cabin** – Phoenix and Jenna

**Take Me To The Lake** – Cash and Hope

**Taken by The Mountain Man** - Cole and Jana

**Take Me To The Mountain** – Bennett and Willow

**Take Me To The Edge** – Storm

**Mountain Men of Mustang Mountain**

**February is for Ford** – Ford and Luna

**April is for Asher** – Asher and Jenna

**Club Red – Short Stories**
**Daddy's Dare** – Knox and Summer
**Sold to my Ex's Dad** - Evan and Jana
**Jingling His Bells** – Zion and Emma

**Club Red: Chicago**
**Elusive Dom**

**Chasing the Sun Duet**
**Sunrise** – Kade and Lin
**Sunset** – Jasper and Brynn

**Rock Stars of Nashville**
**She's Still The One** – Dallas and Austin

**Standalone Books**
**Texting Titan** - Denver and Avery
**Accidental Sugar Daddy** – Owen and Ellie
**Stay With Me Now** – David and Ivy
**Midnight Rose** - Ruby and Orlando
**Committed Cowboy** – Whiskey Run Cowboys
**Stalking His Obsession** - Dakota and Grant
**Falling in Love on Route 66** - Weston and Rory

**Billionaire's Marigold -** Mari and Dalton

**A Baby for Her Best Friend** – Nick and Summer

# CONNECT WITH KACI ROSE

Website
Facebook
Kaci Rose Reader's Facebook Group
TikTok
Instagram
Twitter
Goodreads
Book Bub
Join Kaci Rose's VIP List (Newsletter)

# ABOUT KACI ROSE

Kaci Rose writes steamy contemporary romance mostly set in small towns. She grew up in Florida but longs for the mountains over the beach.

She is a mom to 5 kids, a dog who is scared of his own shadow, and a puppy who's actively destroying her house.

She also writes steamy cowboy romance as Kaci M. Rose.

## PLEASE LEAVE A REVIEW!

I love to hear from my readers! Please **head over to your favorite store and leave a review** of what you thought of this book!

Made in the USA
Columbia, SC
24 September 2024

42937287R00063